What is Lila hiding?

"Lila!" Jessica said, putting down her tuna sandwich. She couldn't understand why Lila didn't want to come to their camp-out. "What's the matter?"

"Nothing," Lila muttered. She sipped her milk and didn't say anything else.

"She's a scaredy-cat; that's what's wrong with her," Charlie teased. "She's afraid of the dark."

Lila thumped her milk carton down on the table. "I am not!"

Winston raised his eyebrows. "Maybe she's afraid of ghosts!"

"Or maybe she wets her bed," Charlie said, laughing.

Lila turned beet red.

Bantam Books in the SWEET VALLEY KIDS series

SWEET VALLEY KIDS

LILA'S SECRET

Written by
Molly Mia Stewart

Created by
FRANCINE PASCAL

Illustrated by
Ying-Hwa Hu

BANTAM BOOKS
NEW YORK · TORONTO · LONDON · SYDNEY · AUCKLAND

RL 2, 005–008

LILA'S SECRET
A Bantam Book / April 1990

*Sweet Valley High® and Sweet Valley Kids® are
registered trademarks of Francine Pascal*

Conceived by Francine Pascal

*Produced by Daniel Weiss Associates, Inc.
33 West 17th Street
New York, NY 10011*

Cover art by James Mathewuse.

ISBN 0-553-56732-2

Published simultaneously in the United States and Canada

*Bantam Books are published by Bantam Books, a division of Bantam
Doubleday Dell Publishing Group, Inc. Its trademark, consisting of the
words "Bantam Books" and the portrayal of a rooster, is Registered in U.S.
Patent and Trademark Office and in other countries. Marca Registrada.
Bantam Books, 1540 Broadway, New York, New York, 10036.*

PRINTED IN THE UNITED STATES OF AMERICA

OPM   0 9 8 7 6 5 4 3 2 1

To Briana Ferris Adler

CHAPTER 1

The Hideout

Jessica and Elizabeth Wakefield and Elizabeth's friend Amy Sutton were playing outside in the Wakefields' backyard one afternoon after school.

"This can be our emergency escape door," Elizabeth said as she opened the flaps of a giant cardboard box. "See?"

Jessica, who was Elizabeth's identical twin, poked at the box with one finger. "You mean I have to crawl through it?" she asked uncertainly.

"Sure!" Elizabeth said, nodding. "It has to

be small so we won't be seen by our ene-mies."

The girls were making a fort. They had gathered several large cardboard boxes, some pieces of wood from the garage, and an old blanket. Elizabeth was having a great time, but she could tell Jessica wasn't enjoy-ing herself very much. Jessica didn't like to do messy, outdoor things. Most of the time, Jessica wanted to play inside with their big dollhouse, and Elizabeth wanted to be out-side playing horses or pirates.

They were different in other ways, too. Elizabeth loved reading stories and even writing some of her own. She liked going to school and learning new things. Jessica thought the best part about school was whis-pering to her friends and passing notes. She didn't like doing homework either, but Elizabeth almost always helped her. Even though Elizabeth and Jessica were identical twins, they weren't identical on the inside.

On the outside the girls looked exactly alike. Both of them had long blond hair and bright blue-green eyes and were exactly the same size. When they wore matching outfits to school, no one in their second-grade class could tell them apart. The only way to be sure who was who was to check their name bracelets. Being identical twins was fun, because they were also best friends.

"Come on, try out our fort," Elizabeth said to Jessica. "You can crawl inside."

Jessica shook her head. "You do it first. Or Amy can."

Amy was Elizabeth's best friend after Jessica. She loved to do all the same things

3

Elizabeth did and she was having fun help-
ing with the fort.

"OK," Amy said. Her knees were already
dirty from crawling on the ground. She
pushed the flaps open and scrambled into the big box. "I'm going all the way inside!"

Elizabeth poked her head in to watch her
friend. Amy crawled on her stomach through
to the other side and pushed the flaps open.
Then she disappeared.

"Where are you?" Elizabeth shouted.

"I'm in here!" Amy's voice was coming
from the thick bushes. "Come on! It's fun in
here!"

Elizabeth looked at her sister. "Follow me,
Jess. It's not scary."

"I'm not scared," Jessica said. She shrugged,
and began to smile. "OK, let's go."

Together, Elizabeth and Jessica crawled through the big box. At the other end, Amy was kneeling down to watch them come out.

"This is neat!" Elizabeth said as she stood up. They were in a hollow area inside the bushes. It was just like a cave. Over their heads were branches and green leaves, and Elizabeth could see little pieces of sky through the tangled branches.

Jessica was turning around and around. "This is kind of scary, too!"

"Wouldn't it be fun to stay in here all day?" Amy said. She pointed to one side. "There's a place over there that's like a separate room. This could be our hideout!"

Elizabeth nodded. "You know what?" she whispered.

The others looked at her. "What?" Jessica asked.

"We could sleep out in here!" Elizabeth liked her idea so much she couldn't stop smiling. "Wouldn't that be fun?"

"Yes!" Amy gasped. "That's a great idea!"

Jessica wrinkled up her nose. "But it's kind of icky in here," she said. She checked the ground for bugs. "I wouldn't want to be here at night. It would be so damp."

"Then how about in our tent?" Elizabeth sat down on the ground. "We could invite Eva and Lila and Ellen," she went on. They were the twins' other close friends.

"You mean have a camp-out?" Amy asked excitedly. "Don't you want to, Jessica? It would be so much fun!"

"Well . . . if it's in a tent . . ." she began.

"It would be," Elizabeth promised. "It would be nice and dry and with no bugs."

Jessica smiled. "Well . . ." she said. "We've never had a sleepover before, so let's have a sleepover camp-out!"

CHAPTER 2
A Secret Meeting

Jessica and Elizabeth raced all the way to class the next morning. In the doorway, Jessica bumped into Andy Franklin. His books toppled onto the floor, and then his glasses fell off.

"Oops! Sorry!" Jessica giggled. Elizabeth stopped to help him pick everything up. "Come on," Jessica said. She grabbed her twin sister's hand. "Lila and Ellen are over there!"

Jessica dragged Elizabeth into the classroom. She could already see Lila Fowler, her best friend after Elizabeth, and Ellen Riteman, standing next to the hamster cage.

"Hey, everyone," Amy said, running to catch up to Elizabeth and Jessica. "Did your mom and dad say yes?"

Jessica nodded three times. "Yup! This Saturday."

"Can you come?" Elizabeth asked.

Amy grinned. "Sure. It'll be so much fun."

"Come on," Jessica said. She was impatient to ask their other friends and led the way to the other side of the room. Elizabeth waved to Eva Simpson to tell her to come over, too.

"Listen," Jessica began when they were all standing together. She looked over her shoulder and then lowered her voice. "This is a secret meeting."

Lila opened her brown eyes wide. She loved secrets. "What is it?" she whispered.

"We're having a—" Jessica began. Then she stopped because she saw Caroline Pearce standing nearby. Caroline was a busybody, and Jessica was sure she was listening in.

With one finger on her lips, Jessica tiptoed a few steps away. The others followed her. "We're having a camp-out," she announced. "Can you all come?"

"A camp-out?" Ellen said loudly. She put one hand over her mouth and giggled. "Wow!"

Eva nodded excitedly. "I love camping!"

"It's just in our backyard," Elizabeth told them. "But our mom said we can have a cookout, too."

Jessica was waiting for Lila to say yes. "Won't it be fun, Lila?" she asked.

11

Lila's face turned pink. "I think I'm supposed to sleep at my grandmother's that night," she said.

"But you don't even know what night it's going to be," Elizabeth pointed out.

"Well . . ." Lila began slowly.

"What night are you going to your grandmother's?" Jessica asked.

Lila's face got even pinker. She looked down at the floor. "Umm . . . Friday?"

"Our camp-out is Saturday," Elizabeth said.

"So you can come," Jessica added happily.

Lila began twisting one of the buttons on her shirt. "I'm not sure. What if it rains?"

"We'll be in the tent!" Amy reminded her.

"Or, we could sleep inside the house if it rains really hard," Elizabeth added.

"But what about bugs?" Lila said. "On the ground."

Ellen shrugged. "We'll be in our sleeping bags."

"Don't you want to go?" Eva asked in a puzzled voice.

"It's just—" Lila chewed on a piece of her hair. "I'll have to ask permission. My parents are very strict."

Jessica's mouth dropped open. That wasn't true at all! Lila's parents let her do almost anything she wanted.

"Just say yes, Lila," Jessica pleaded. "It'll be fun. I promise."

"Come on, Lila. Say yes," Ellen added.

Lila shrugged. "Well, maybe." She didn't sound very positive.

"Come on, Lila!" a voice interrupted.

Jessica and the others turned around. Winston Egbert and Todd Wilkins were standing behind them. They were both trying not to laugh.

"Quit spying on us! This is a secret meeting," Jessica said angrily.

Todd's brown eyes looked mischievous. "We didn't hear anything, right, Win?"

"Right," Winston agreed. Then both of them laughed again and walked away.

Jessica looked at her sister. If the boys heard about their camp-out, that could mean trouble!

CHAPTER 3

Lila's Idea

Elizabeth and Jessica walked through the big double doors of the Sweet Valley Dance Studio that afternoon. They each carried a large zippered bag with polka dots, but Elizabeth's was green and Jessica's was pink. They were right on time for their modern dance class.

They went into the crowded dressing room where other girls were changing into leotards and tights.

"Hi, Jessica. Hi, Elizabeth," Ellen greeted

them. Lila was facing the mirror, brushing her hair.

"Hi, everyone," Jessica said.

Lila put her brush down and came over to the twins. "You know what?" she said. She was wearing a brand-new leotard with a leopard print pattern.

Elizabeth put her bag down. "What?"

"What?" Jessica repeated. She sat down on the floor beside her bag and began unpacking her dance clothes.

"I have a really good idea," Lila said. "About the camp-out."

Elizabeth's stomach flip-flopped. "Uh-oh," she said in a low voice. When Lila said that, it usually meant a really good idea for Lila but not for anyone else.

Lila straightened her leg warmers. She

17

kept looking at the floor while she spoke. "Maybe we could have the camp-out at my house," she said.

"Why?" Elizabeth gasped. "It was *our* idea to have a camp-out!"

"That's right," Jessica said. She looked at her friend in surprise. "We thought of it!"

Lila shrugged, and her cheeks started to turn pink. "But it would be better at my house," she explained. "I have a pool."

"So do we!" Jessica said stubbornly. Her cheeks were pink, too. Elizabeth knew her sister was upset.

Ellen was looking from Lila to Jessica to Lila again.

"Mine's a real pool," Lila pointed out.

"That's true," Ellen said, nodding.

"Our pool is just as real as yours," Elizabeth shot back angrily. Lila always wanted

everything her own way. Sometimes Elizabeth wished Jessica didn't like Lila so much.

"So, your pool is in the ground and ours is above the ground," Jessica said. "Our pool is just as good as yours."

Ellen nodded again. "That's true."

"But we have a pool house," Lila went on. "Screened in and everything. There's a TV and a VCR. We could watch any movie we want."

"Wow!" Ellen gasped. Her eyes widened. "Could we?"

"But we're going camping!" Elizabeth said. "You're not supposed to watch TV on a campout."

Ellen looked at Lila and nodded. "She's right, Lila."

Jessica glared at Ellen and then stared at Lila. "And we're camping out at *our* house."

No one said anything for a few seconds. It was so quiet that Elizabeth could hear her heart beating. Everyone else had already left the dressing room.

Lila's face was bright pink. "It was just an *idea*," she said, almost in tears. She ran out of the dressing room. Ellen followed her.

Elizabeth was surprised. She had never seen Lila so upset before. "I wonder what's bothering her," Elizabeth said.

"Why does she have to act that way?" Jessica grumbled as she finished changing into her leotard.

Elizabeth frowned while she put her hair in a ponytail. "Maybe she's afraid she'll be homesick."

"Lila?" Jessica made a face. "Not her."

"Then why doesn't she want to sleep over at our house?" Elizabeth wondered.

"She just wants everything her way," Jessica said angrily.

But Elizabeth had a feeling it was more than that. She was certain Lila was worried about something—but what could it be?

CHAPTER 4

Lila's Secret

Jessica put her lunch bag down on the cafeteria table and sat down in a chair next to Elizabeth. "What did we get today?" she asked.

"Tuna squish," Elizabeth replied. That was their name for tuna fish.

"I'll trade you for bologna," Winston Egbert said, leaning across the table. He was sitting between Todd Wilkins and Ken Matthews. Next to Ken sat Charlie Cashman, who blew the paper off his straw at Lois Waller.

Jessica examined Winston's sandwich and wrinkled her nose. "I only eat bologna with nothing else on it. Just plain."

"Mine's got mustard." Winston sighed. "Hey, quit it!" he yelled as Charlie tried to grab his banana.

"Yuck, bologna," Lila said with a shiver. "That stuff is horrible."

"Yuck, that stuff is horrible," Charlie repeated in a high voice. He smiled at Lila with food showing between his teeth.

Jessica pretended Charlie wasn't there. He was always teasing her.

"We know what you girls are doing this weekend," Todd announced. He grinned at Elizabeth.

Elizabeth opened her eyes wide and gave Jessica a pretend puzzled look. "What is he talking about?" she asked.

24

"I don't know," Jessica replied, trying hard not to smile. "We aren't doing anything special this weekend. Right, Lila?"

Lila didn't answer. Instead she took a big sip of her milk.

"Well, *we're* going to do something special," Todd announced. He looked up at the ceiling. "If anyone happens to be camping out, they might get raided. But I guess it won't be anyone at this table."

"No!" Jessica screamed. She didn't want the boys to ruin their plans. "Don't you dare, Todd Wilkins!" she added with a giggle.

Winston, Ken, and Charlie all started laughing. "What are you afraid of?" Charlie asked. "You just said you weren't doing anything."

Lila blinked several times, as if she were

going to cry. She looked at Jessica and gulped. "Forget it. I'm not coming now."

"Lila!" Jessica put down her tuna sandwich and gave her friend a serious look. She couldn't understand why Lila didn't want to camp out with them. "What's the matter?"

"Nothing," Lila muttered. She sipped her milk and didn't say anything else.

"She's a scaredy-cat; that's what's wrong with her," Charlie teased. "She's afraid of the dark."

Lila thumped her milk carton down on the table. "I am not!"

Winston raised his eyebrows. "Maybe she's afraid of ghosts!"

Todd and Ken laughed loudly. "Wooo-ooo-oo!" Ken said in a spooky voice.

"Maybe she's afraid of wild animals!" Todd laughed.

26

"I am not!" Lila shouted.

"Why don't you want to sleep outside, Lila?" Charlie said with a grin. "Do you snore?"

Lila was getting more and more angry. "I don't snore, Charlie Cashman," Lila growled.

Charlie held his hands up and looked at the other boys. "What's wrong, then? Do you wet your bed?"

All of the boys went into wild whoops of laughter. Jessica rolled her eyes. "You guys are so dumb," she told them in her most grown-up voice. She wished she knew the real reason why Lila didn't want to come.

"Yeah. Cut it out," Elizabeth chimed in. "You're being mean."

Lila was now beet red. Jessica had never

seen her looking so upset. Usually, no one could tease Lila and get away with it.

"We'll find out your secret, Lila," Winston said, laughing. "If anyone is having a camp-out, that is."

Jessica looked at her sister. She felt a little bit like laughing, too. She couldn't wait to find out if the boys were really going to play any tricks on them!

CHAPTER 5

Backyard Fun

"OK, kids!" Mr. Wakefield announced. "Let's get this tent open!"

Elizabeth ran to help her father. It was Saturday afternoon, and their friends would be arriving soon. "I'll unroll it, Dad. Come on, Jess."

Elizabeth and Jessica unrolled the large canvas tent. It had strings and flaps and zippers all over it.

"P-U!" Jessica said. She made a face and held her nose. "This has a stinky smell."

Their father began putting stakes in the ground. "That's why we're putting it up now, so it can air out."

"This is so much better than our fort. I'm going inside," Elizabeth announced. The tent was only partway up, but she crawled in anyway, and Jessica followed her. "This is going to be so much fun!"

Their older brother, Steven, poked his head through the flap. "Hey, you'd better check out the sleeping bags," he warned. "There could be snakes in them."

Jessica screeched, but Elizabeth stuck her tongue out at her brother. "Very funny, Steven."

"There wouldn't be," Jessica asked fearfully, "would there?"

Elizabeth shook her head no and crawled

outside. Steven was unzipping one of the sleeping bags. "Look out!" he yelled. "There's a giant spider!"

Jessica ran across the lawn and climbed up onto the picnic table. "Get it away from me!"

"There're no spiders," Elizabeth said. Very carefully, she opened the sleeping bag Steven had dropped. She took a deep breath and pulled it all the way open. "No spiders," she announced. She gave Steven a mean look but spoiled it by giggling.

Mrs. Wakefield came out of the house and walked over to where the tent was being set up.

"Now, let's talk about rules," she said. "I don't want any fighting. And no fooling around." Mr. Wakefield looked surprised. "Well, not *too* much fooling around," Mrs. Wakefield added with a smile.

Elizabeth and Jessica shared a look of excitement. Their camp-out was going to be so much fun!

Eva arrived at the Wakefields' house at five o'clock. She was carrying a pillow, a stuffed horse, and a brand-new sleeping bag that still had the tags on it. "This is my first sleeping bag," she explained. "We bought it today."

"I like your horse," Jessica told her. "It's pretty."

Eva hugged it tight. "Her name is Arabella. I always sleep with her."

"That's a nice name," Elizabeth said.

A few minutes later, Amy and Ellen arrived. The girls went into the tent to arrange their sleeping bags. "I'm sleeping next to Liz," Jessica told everyone. She looked around. "It's crowded in here."

Amy giggled and switched her flashlight

on and off. "We're like sardines." She turned the flashlight on and held it under her chin so it shone up into her face. It made her look like a monster. "Wooo-oooo!" she moaned.

"That's neat!" Elizabeth said. She was so excited, she could hardly wait for it to be nighttime.

"Girls!" Mrs. Wakefield called. "Lila's here!"

One by one, the girls popped out of the tent door and tumbled onto the grass. Lila was carrying an armload of things. She even had a small suitcase.

"We weren't sure you were coming," Elizabeth said.

"You're just in time," Jessica added.

Lila dropped everything on the ground in front of the tent. "I brought my sleeping bag, clothes for tomorrow, a pillow, an extra blanket, bug spray, a raincoat, and a few other things," she said.

Jessica shook her head. "That's going to fill up the whole tent!" she said. She pointed to a small paper bag next to Lila's suitcase. "What's in there?"

"Nothing!" Lila picked it up and hid it behind her back. "It's just some stuff," she mumbled.

Elizabeth was more sure than ever that Lila was worried about something. She remembered how upset Lila had been when the boys were teasing her. Now she seemed to be hiding something.

"Time to start dinner!" Mrs. Wakefield announced.

"I want a hot dog!" Jessica shouted. Ellen and Amy both said, "Me, too!"

Mrs. Wakefield put a big platter of hamburgers and hot dogs next to the grill. "I'll make some of each, and everyone can have what they want."

Soon each girl's paper plate was piled high with potato chips, carrot sticks, hamburgers, hot dogs, and watermelon. Elizabeth helped pour juice into paper cups.

"I don't want any," Lila told her. "I'm not thirsty."

"I am," Amy said. Her throat went *glug-glug-glug* while she gulped down her juice. "Can I have another cup?"

Everyone was thirsty but Lila. She shook her head when Mrs. Wakefield offered to give her milk, water, or soda, instead.

"Watch this," Eva called. She took two of her watermelon seeds and pressed them on her forehead. They stuck to her skin.

"They look like giant freckles." Elizabeth

giggled. She stuck watermelon seeds on her cheeks. "They feel funny!"

Ellen spit a seed out, and it landed on Jessica's foot.

"Hey!" Jessica shrieked. She spit a seed at Ellen, and then ran away laughing.

"I'll get you!" Ellen said. Elizabeth had two seeds in her mouth, and she spit them at Amy.

The girls tried to hit one another with watermelon seeds for a while.

Then, they played freeze tag, red-light green-light, and sardines. Soon it began to get dark.

"Time to change into your pj's, girls," Mrs. Wakefield said as she came out of the house. "And then, everybody, into your sleeping bags!"

The girls jumped up and down with delight.

The camp-out was about to begin!

CHAPTER 6

Lights Out!

Jessica jumped down off the picnic bench. "Last one in is a rotten string bean!" she shouted. The girls raced to the tent, bumping into one another and giggling in the darkness.

Inside, Amy and Lila turned on their flashlights, so it was bright enough to see. Jessica wriggled into her sleeping bag and flopped onto her back. "I bet I'll never fall asleep," she said.

Eva unzipped her sleeping bag. "I bet you will."

"Aren't you going to put on your pajamas?" Elizabeth asked Jessica.

Jessica clapped one hand over her mouth. "Oops! I forgot."

For a few minutes, everyone was busy putting on their nightgowns and pajamas. Then Ellen took an old stuffed rabbit out of her duffel bag and set it down on her pillow. Eva was hugging her horse, Arabella, and Amy had a teddy bear with one eye missing. Jessica was glad she had brought her koala bear outside to sleep with. Elizabeth had a koala bear, too. The only one without a cuddly toy was Lila.

"Don't you have a bear or something?" Jessica asked her.

Lila was carefully arranging all of her belongings. She shook her head. "I'm too big for that," she said.

39

"Not me," Ellen said firmly. "I always sleep with Bugsy."

"Should we turn off our flashlights?" Amy asked.

Elizabeth nodded. Jessica could see she was smiling. "Yes," Elizabeth said. "Let's see how dark it is."

Lila and Amy both clicked off the lights. Suddenly, the tent was completely dark. Jessica blinked and waved her hand in front of her face, but she couldn't see anything! It was very quiet all of a sudden, too.

"It sure is dark in here," Eva said after a minute.

Jessica nodded, even though she knew no one could see her. She turned so she was facing her sister. It was getting easier to see in the dark. Elizabeth looked like a long lump beside her. "Are you scared?" Jessica whispered.

"No," Elizabeth whispered back.

Jessica gulped hard. "Me, neither," she said. But she wasn't so sure.

It was quiet again for a little while. "Do you think the boys will really come?" Ellen asked in a loud whisper.

"If they do, I won't be scared," Amy whispered back.

"Me, neither," Elizabeth said.

Jessica hugged her koala bear tight. "They can't scare us."

Cree-cree! Cree-cree! came a noise.

"What was that?" Lila cried. She sat straight up in her sleeping bag.

Jessica reached her hand out to Elizabeth. Elizabeth took her hand and squeezed it. "It's just crickets," Elizabeth said.

"I wish I was in my own bed," Ellen said.

She sounded unhappy. "I've never slept away from home before."

Jessica squeezed her sister's hand. It was a little bit scary sleeping outside, even in their own backyard. Being with Elizabeth made her feel a lot better, though.

"I wonder if the boys will come," Lila said, sounding worried.

Elizabeth sat up on her knees. "We're not allowed to sneak over to someone's house at night," she said. "I'll bet boys aren't, either."

"Not Todd," Jessica reminded her. "He lives just a few blocks away."

There was silence for a few moments.

"Todd wouldn't play tricks on us," Elizabeth said, after a moment. She didn't sound very sure, though.

Jessica squirmed in her sleeping bag to move closer to her sister.

"You know what?" Eva said. "There could be wild animals out there."

Amy giggled. "There aren't any wild animals around here. Just cats and dogs."

Jessica laughed. She was glad Amy said that.

"But you know what there could be?" Amy went on in a spooky voice. "There could be ghosts."

Ellen, Lila, and Eva screamed at once. Jessica screamed, too, but then said, "You're being silly. There's no such thing as ghosts."

"Oh, yeah?" Amy said. "I heard a story about—"

Just then, there was a sharp *crack* outside the tent!

Jessica gasped. "Somebody's out there!"

43

CHAPTER 7

Who's Out There?

"Oh, no!" Eva wailed from her sleeping bag. "I think it's raining! Arabella will get soaked!"

There was a pitter-patter sound on the top of the tent. Elizabeth's heart thumped hard.

"Rain! What if it comes through the tent!" Ellen cried.

Everyone quickly unzipped their sleeping bags and began to get up. "I'm stuck!" Amy yelled as she tugged at her zipper.

Jessica grabbed her koala bear and her

pillow. "We'll have to go inside, everyone. We'll get wet if we don't."

Outside, the rain was still splashing down on the tent. But Elizabeth was puzzled. She noticed that it only seemed to be raining on one side of the tent. While the others were feeling around in the dark for their shoes, Elizabeth poked her head out of the tent.

Two people were outside, holding a hose and spraying water right on the tent! "Hey!" Elizabeth shouted. She picked up the flashlight next to her and shone it on them. It was Steven and Todd! Steven dropped the hose when she saw them. "Hi, Liz," he said quickly.

"Stop it, you guys!" Elizabeth said angrily. "It's not funny." She crawled out the tent door and stood up.

"You all thought it was raining!" Steven

laughed. He and Todd doubled up with laughter. "You girls were really screaming in there!"

Elizabeth looked inside the tent again. "It's Todd and Steven," she told the others. "They're trying to scare us."

Steven picked up the hose again, and waved it in the air. The spray of water almost hit Elizabeth. "Cut it out, Steven!" she yelled.

The other girls came out of the tent. "Stop being so mean!" Lila shouted. "You've ruined everything! I knew this camp-out was a dumb idea!"

Ellen's chin was quivering. "I want to go home," she said.

"This is just water," Steven said. "See?" He waved the hose toward them again, spraying the ground a few feet from where the girls were standing. But the hose wiggled out of his hand and sent a long shower of water all over Ellen. She screamed and started crying.

"What's going on out here?" Mr. Wakefield's voice boomed across the backyard. All the outdoor lights came on as the back door opened. Mr. and Mrs. Wakefield came outside in their bathrobes.

"Dad! Mom! Steven and Todd were trying to scare us!" Jessica said, running across the lawn to them. "Then Amy couldn't get out of her sleeping bag, and Ellen got soaked, and we're really mad at Steven and Todd!"

Ellen began to cry. "I'm calling my mom."

Elizabeth looked over at Todd. His face was red, and he looked like he felt sorry for what he had done. He looked at Elizabeth and shrugged his shoulders.

Mrs. Wakefield walked closer. "Is that you, Todd Wilkins?"

"Yes, ma'am," Todd said nervously.

Steven was trying to turn the hose off. He looked very embarrassed.

"Mom! Isn't Steven going to get in trouble?" Jessica asked.

Ellen kept crying. "I want to go home!" she repeated.

"Now listen, everyone!" Mr. Wakefield said. He looked sternly at the boys. "The excitement's over. Let's all go back to bed. First, though, I'm going to walk Todd home."

Todd stared at the ground. Elizabeth felt bad that he and Steven were going to get in trouble. She had been a little scared at first, but nothing bad had happened. She walked over to him.

"I'm not mad at you," she whispered in his ear.

Todd smiled and looked at the ground. "Thanks, Liz," he said.

"Come on, Todd," Mr. Wakefield said.

"And Steven, go inside right now," Mrs. Wakefield said. "We'll talk about this in the morning."

Elizabeth looked over at the tent. Sleeping bags had been dragged partway outside, and one side of the tent was sagging. Water was still dripping from it, too.

"I want to go home!" Ellen sobbed for the third time. She was hiccuping and sniffling and hugging her rabbit.

Amy, Eva, and Lila stood together in a bunch. They looked very unhappy and sleepy.

The camp-out was ruined.

CHAPTER 8

Lila's Paper Bag

"Ellen," Mrs. Wakefield said gently. "Would you like to go home?"
Ellen looked like she was going to cry again. "Yes. I miss my mom!"

Jessica looked at her sister and shook her head. Elizabeth shook her head, too. They both felt bad for Ellen. Jessica wondered if *she* would have cried if she were sleeping at someone else's house.

"Why don't we call your mother on the phone?" Mrs. Wakefield suggested to Ellen.

"Then we'll see how you feel. Would you like that?"

Ellen's lower lip trembled and she nodded.

"OK," Mrs. Wakefield said, smiling. She held out her hand to Ellen. "Let's go call your mom. We'll find you some dry pajamas, too."

"Come on," Elizabeth said to the others. She headed back to the tent.

"Do we have to go back in?" Lila whined.

Amy kneeled in front of the tent and poked her head inside. Jessica and the others could see she was patting the sleeping bags and the ground. "It's not wet," she called out.

"I'm coming in," Eva said, crawling inside.

Lila looked at the ground for a few seconds. Then she followed them.

"Come on, Jess," Elizabeth said. They went into the tent. Eva and Amy were both hugging their animals.

"Boy, I'm so mad at those boys," Lila grumbled, as she turned on her flashlight.

Jessica shrugged. "Me, too, I guess." She looked at Elizabeth and they grinned at each other. The boys' raid had made the camp-out even more exciting.

There was a rustling noise outside, and Ellen came back in. She was holding her rabbit, and she looked much happier.

"Did you call your mom?" Eva asked.

Ellen nodded. "Yup," she said, stepping carefully over Lila, Jessica, and Elizabeth. She sat down on her sleeping bag, hugged her rabbit and kissed him good night.

"I'm sure glad I brought Bugsy with me," she said.

"Me, too," Amy said. "I'm glad I brought Mr. Golly."

"Mr. Golly?" Jessica repeated. She giggled.

"That's a cute name." She kissed her koala bear.

"I think you're all silly," Lila said.

Elizabeth frowned. "Just because you don't need a teddy bear doesn't mean you have to tease anyone else."

"Yeah," Eva said.

Lila made a face. "I'm turning off the flashlight now," she said in a loud voice.

It was completely dark again. While Jessica waited for her eyes to get used to the dark, she thought she heard a soft, crumpling noise.

Jessica's heart beat fast. Was there something outside?

Slowly, Jessica felt around in the dark for the flashlight. The sound began again just as she touched the flashlight. She sat up quickly and switched it on.

"Lila!" she gasped.

Lila was reaching into the paper bag she wouldn't let anyone see before. She blinked in the bright light and looked surprised.

Ellen sat up. "What is it?" she whispered.

Jessica shone the light on Lila's bag. "What's in that bag?" she asked.

Lila looked angry and scared at the same time. She pulled an old blanket out of the bag. "It's just my blankie," she muttered.

"Blankie?" Amy said, hugging Mr. Golly. "Now that's a silly name."

"It sure is," Ellen said. "I thought you didn't need something to sleep with."

"I only sleep with it when I'm not in my own bed," Lila explained. She sounded like she might cry.

Jessica was surprised. "Is that why you didn't want to sleep over?" she asked. "Because you didn't want us to know that you still slept with a blankie."

The tent was very quiet. Lila wouldn't look at any of them. Then she nodded. "I guess so," she said.

"Well, now we know, so good night," said Jessica. She lay down and switched off the flashlight.

In a few moments, the tent was completely quiet again. Jessica, Elizabeth, Eva, Amy, and Ellen all snuggled in their sleeping bags. Only Lila stayed awake.

CHAPTER 9

Lila's Big Secret

When Elizabeth opened her eyes, it looked like it was still the middle of the night. She wondered how long she had been asleep. She wondered what woke her up.

Then she heard what sounded like someone crying.

Elizabeth sat up in her sleeping bag. The tent was very dark, but she could see the shapes of her friends in their sleeping bags. On the other side of Jessica, Lila was curled up in a tight ball. She was sniffling and crying quietly.

"Lila?" Elizabeth called out softly. "Lila?"

The crying stopped, but Lila didn't answer.

"Lila?" Elizabeth called again. "What's wrong?"

Slowly, Lila uncurled and sat up. Elizabeth couldn't see her face, but Lila's shoulders were shaking.

"I can't tell you," Lila said in a choking voice.

Elizabeth felt worried. She sat up on her knees and leaned over her sister. "What's wrong?" she asked again.

Lila sniffed. She was rubbing the inside of her sleeping bag with something. "I didn't mean to," she whispered, shaking her head.

"Mean to what?" Elizabeth was very confused.

Jessica rolled over in her sleeping bag. "What is it?" she whispered.

Lila began to cry again. She stood up and began to drag her sleeping bag out the tent door. Elizabeth and Jessica crawled outside behind her.

"What's wrong with Lila?" Jessica whispered to Elizabeth. Elizabeth shrugged but she was starting to get an idea. She remembered how angry Lila had become when the boys had teased her at lunch. She also remembered that Lila wouldn't drink anything at dinnertime.

She tiptoed to Lila and whispered in her ear. "Did you wet your sleeping bag?"

Lila let out a *boo hoo* and nodded. "I didn't mean to!"

"What?" Jessica gasped. "You *did*?"

"Don't tell anyone!" Lila sniffled. "I only do it when I sleep away from home!"

Everything made sense now. "So, that's the real reason why you didn't want to sleep over, right?" Elizabeth asked. She felt very bad for Lila.

Lila nodded. She looked from Elizabeth to Jessica with a frightened expression. "You won't tell, will you?"

"I promise," Elizabeth said quickly. She crossed her heart and snapped her fingers twice. That was the special promise sign the Wakefield family used.

"What about you, Jessica? Do you promise?" Lila asked with concern. She knew she could trust Elizabeth to keep her secret, but she wasn't so sure about Jessica.

"Well," Jessica began teasingly. Lila's eyes

grew wide. "Of course I do," Jessica said, making the promise sign.

"Thanks," Lila said with a sigh of relief.

"Is your sleeping bag all wet?" Elizabeth asked.

Lila shook her head quickly. "It's just a little bit wet. I really hardly ever do it anymore," she said again. "Just sometimes!"

"You know what?" Elizabeth said. "Steven used to do that, too. But Dr. Bartlett said he would grow out of it, and he did!"

"That's right," Jessica added. "He never wet his bed after second grade."

"Really?" Lila sniffled. "I hope I'll stop, too."

Elizabeth nodded. "You will. You know, *I* wet my bed once after watching a scary movie on TV."

"And you really promise you won't tell anyone? Ever?" Lila begged.

Elizabeth smiled. "Promise."

"Promise," Jessica repeated. She yawned a big yawn. "Let's go back to sleep now, OK?"

"OK," Lila said. "I'll put my blankie over the wet spot."

"Good idea," Elizabeth said. She led the way to the tent. "I can't wait to go to sleep, because when we wake up, we get to have pancakes for breakfast."

"Then let's hurry up." Jessica giggled. "Last one to get to sleep is a rotten broccoli."

Lila giggled, too, and, pulling her sleeping bag behind her, followed the twins back into the tent.

CHAPTER 10

A Pancake Breakfast

The next time Jessica opened her eyes, it was morning. She squirmed around to face her sister. All she could see was Elizabeth's blond hair poking out of the sleeping bag.

"Liz!" she whispered. "Are you awake?" There was no answer, so Jessica nudged her. "Are you awake?"

Slowly, Elizabeth opened her eyes and pulled the sleeping bag away from her face. She blinked. "Is it time to get up?" she said sleepily.

"I think so," Jessica said. "It's morning."

"Is anyone else awake?" Elizabeth sat up, rubbing her eyes. Then she looked at the lumpy shapes all around the tent. Eva was sleeping on her back, Amy's head was under her pillow, Ellen was still hugging Bugsy tight, and Lila was curled up in a little ball.

"What a bunch of sleepyheads," Jessica giggled. She covered her mouth to keep quiet.

Eva said, "Ahhh," and rolled over onto her side. She got up on her elbows and blinked. "Is it time to get up?" she asked.

Jessica climbed out of her sleeping bag. "Yes," she answered as she unzipped the tent flaps. The noise made Amy sit up very fast. "Who's there?" she called.

The others giggled. "You look pretty funny, Amy," Elizabeth told her.

"Hello, everyone," Ellen said, sitting up

and blinking. "I didn't think I would fall asleep but I did."

"Are you still homesick?" Jessica asked her.

Ellen thought for a moment. Then she smiled and shrugged. "I guess not."

"Lila's still sleeping," Eva said. She reached over to tickle Lila. "Wake up, sleepy-head!"

Lila grumbled as she wiggled around in her sleeping bag. The others started to get up and look for their shoes.

"Is it morning?" Lila asked. Her voice sounded growly and scratchy.

Jessica nodded happily. "Yessireee!"

Lila sat up and stretched. Then she quickly glanced at Jessica and Elizabeth.

Jessica smiled at Lila. Without saying anything, she crossed her heart and snapped her fingers twice. Best friends were supposed to keep secrets, so she would never tell anyone about Lila.

Lila smiled back. "When's breakfast?" she asked cheerfully.

"Right now!" Elizabeth jumped up. Then she climbed out of the tent and shouted, "Last one inside is a rotten cauliflower!"

Jessica screeched and raced after her sister. The others galloped behind. They all tried to get in the back door at once, but they were laughing too hard and kept bumping into one another.

"Whoa! Whoa!" Mr. Wakefield put his hands on the twins' heads. "One at a time!" He held the twins back while their guests went first. Then Jessica and Elizabeth slipped inside.

Mrs. Wakefield was already mixing the

pancake batter. "Good morning, girls! Did you sleep OK after the excitement last night?"

"Yes!" everyone said at the same time.

Jessica looked at Lila, and Lila looked back. They both smiled a secret smile and Lila's face turned pink.

"What's that book?" Eva asked suddenly.

Elizabeth was reading the back cover of one of her books. *"Rabbit's Strange Visitor,"* she said. "It's by my favorite author, Angela Daley."

"I like her books, too," Eva said.

Amy finished her orange juice. "I've read all her books except the second one and the newest one."

"You know what?" Lila waited until everyone was looking at her.

Jessica poked her in the side. "What?"

"Mrs. Becker wrote a letter to Angela Daley," Lila announced. "I saw it on her desk."

"Our teacher, Mrs. Becker?" Elizabeth gasped. "Honest?"

Lila nodded. "Yes. And you know what it said?"

Everyone stared at her. "What?" Ellen asked with excitement.

"It asked if she could come visit our class sometime," Lila told them.

Elizabeth gulped loudly. Her eyes were wide and round. "If Angela Daley came to our school, that would be the best thing in the whole world!"

Will Angela Daley visit Sweet Valley Elementary School? Will Elizabeth get to meet her? Find out in Sweet Valley Kids #7, JESSICA'S BIG MISTAKE.

SWEET VALLEY KIDS

Jessica and Elizabeth have had lots of adventures in *Sweet Valley High* and *Sweet Valley Twins*...now read about the twins at age seven! You'll love all the fun that comes with being seven—birthday parties, playing dress-up, class projects, putting on puppet shows and plays, losing a tooth, setting up lemonade stands, caring for animals and much more! It's all part of SWEET VALLEY KIDS. Read them all!

☐	JESSICA AND THE SPELLING-BEE SURPRISE #21	15917-8	$2.99
☐	SWEET VALLEY SLUMBER PARTY #22	15934-8	$2.99
☐	LILA'S HAUNTED HOUSE PARTY # 23	15919-4	$2.99
☐	COUSIN KELLY'S FAMILY SECRET # 24	15920-8	$2.99
☐	LEFT-OUT ELIZABETH # 25	15921-6	$2.99
☐	JESSICA'S SNOBBY CLUB # 26	15922-4	$2.99
☐	THE SWEET VALLEY CLEANUP TEAM # 27	15923-2	$2.99
☐	ELIZABETH MEETS HER HERO #28	15924-0	$2.99
☐	ANDY AND THE ALIEN # 29	15925-9	$2.99
☐	JESSICA'S UNBURIED TREASURE # 30	15926-7	$2.99
☐	ELIZABETH AND JESSICA RUN AWAY # 31	48004-9	$2.99
☐	LEFT BACK! #32	48005-7	$2.99
☐	CAROLINE'S HALLOWEEN SPELL # 33	48006-5	$2.99
☐	THE BEST THANKSGIVING EVER # 34	48007-3	$2.99
☐	ELIZABETH'S BROKEN ARM # 35	48009-X	$2.99
☐	ELIZABETH'S VIDEO FEVER # 36	48010-3	$2.99
☐	THE BIG RACE # 37	48011-1	$2.99
☐	GOODBYE, EVA? # 38	48012-X	$2.99
☐	ELLEN IS HOME ALONE # 39	48013-8	$2.99
☐	ROBIN IN THE MIDDLE #40	48014-6	$2.99
☐	THE MISSING TEA SET # 41	48015-4	$2.99
☐	JESSICA'S MONSTER NIGHTMARE # 42	48008-1	$2.99
☐	JESSICA GETS SPOOKED # 43	48094-4	$2.99
☐	THE TWINS BIG POW-WOW # 44	48098-7	$2.99
☐	ELIZABETH'S PIANO LESSONS # 45	48102-9	$2.99

Bantam Books, Dept. SVK2, 2451 S. Wolf Road, Des Plaines, IL 60018

Please send me the items I have checked above. I am enclosing $_____ (please add $2.50 to cover postage and handling). Send check or money order, no cash or C.O.D.s please.

Mr/Ms _____

Address _____

City/State _____ Zip _____

SVK2-1/94

Please allow four to six weeks for delivery.
Prices and availability subject to change without notice.

A BANTAM SKYLARK BOOK

FRANCINE PASCAL'S

SWEET VALLEY

Twins AND FRIENDS.®